TINY HANDS

Summer

Creative Activities for Young Children

BARRON'S

Original title of the book in Spanish: *Manitas: Verano*
© Copyright Parramón Ediciones, S.A., 1997—World Rights
Published by Parramón Ediciones, S.A., Barcelona, Spain

Author: Parramón's Editorial Team
Text and Exercises: Anna Galera Bassachs, Mònica Martí i Garbayo, and
Isabel Sanz Muelas
Illustrators: Parramón's Editorial Team
Photographs: Estudio Nos y Soto, AGE Fotostock, Incolor, Fototeca Stone

© Copyright of English edition for the United States, Canada, its territories
and possessions by Barron's Educational Series, Inc. 1999.

All inquiries should be addressed to:
Barron's Educational Series, Inc.
250 Wireless Boulevard
Hauppauge, New York 11788
http://www.barronseduc.com

Library of Congress Catalog Card No.: 98-72537
International Standard Book No. 0-7641-0744-5

Printed in Spain
9 8 7 6 5 4 3 2 1

CONTENTS

INTRODUCTION

The three teachers who wrote this book specialize in early childhood education. They work with children three, four, and five years old, respectively. Because they could not find material for the age groups they were teaching, they decided to compile a book containing a series of activities designed to foster artistic expression and creativity in children. This book provides adults with ideas and strategies for directing each activity so that children can carry them out with the greatest independence—playing, experimenting, and fully enjoying various techniques, thereby progressively acquiring skills and self-sufficiency.

Creative Expression in Preschoolers

Children in this age group have a great deal of curiosity and a desire to discover everything around them. Their thought processes are based on meaningful learning—comprehensive learning that allows children to relate what they already know to the new information they are learning. This type of learning allows children to get to know and interpret, use, and evaluate their surroundings.

In order to promote this process, the activities in this book have a global focus. Why do we use a global focus? Children cannot separate the parts from the whole and cannot take a single piece of information out of its context, but, rather, perceive various stimuli and sensations at once.

The teacher must have different tools and strategies available to relate each handcrafted piece with the various parts of the curriculum. At the end of each activity, therefore, we provide guidelines to help globalize the activity. When carrying out activities, the teacher must not forget the importance of seeing that the children practice habits of cleanliness, neatness, and personal hygiene, reinforcing their sense of independence.

Cognitive activity through direct observation—such as the handling of objects and experimentation—must be stimulated at this stage. The activities presented here allow children to gain new knowledge through discovery.

Artistic creativity is a part of all educational processes and is found in all daily activities and situations. Art is an excellent medium of expression. The various works created by the child can provide a great deal of information about that child.

—Anna Galera Bassachs, Mònica Martí i Garbayo, and Isabel Sanz Muelas

Techniques Used

The different techniques to be found in this book, listed below, are those best suited and most commonly used for this age group.

Hole punching: *You need a felt pad and an awl or fine hole puncher. A series of consecutive holes must be punched along previously drawn lines in order to punch out the desired figure, without tearing the paper with the awl or hole puncher or ripping the paper with your fingers.*

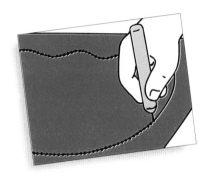

Cutting: *Hold the scissors correctly in one hand while holding the paper with the other. Move the paper along with the scissors and follow the outlines.*

Gluing: *Use only the amount of glue needed for the surfaces to be glued. If the area is large, spread the glue on the paper and simply place the cut-out pieces on top. If it is small, place the piece to be pasted on the glue stick and spread it with glue, then paste it onto the paper.*

Tearing using fingers: *This should be done slowly and carefully, pinching the paper between your fingers.*

Modeling with plasticine: *To cover a flat surface, take a pinch of clay and spread it with your thumb. Some pressure will be required to make the plasticine stick to the surface of the oaktag. Whenever you use plasticine, it should always be varnished afterward to fix it in place and make it shiny and hard.*

Modeling with clay: *The clay must be kneaded well before using it to remove any air bubbles and avoid possible cracks later. It is important to wet the clay with water when joining separate pieces, getting rid of cracks and giving a smooth finish. It is a good idea to paint or varnish the piece once it has dried to give it a smoother finish.*

Painting: *Use wax crayons or clay and fingers, hands, or paintbrushes. When using a paint-brush, remove any excess water to avoid dripping and lumps.*

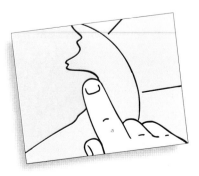

Making stamps: *Stamps can be made of various materials (potatoes, sponges, corks, fingers, hands, and so on). The best way to cover these stamps in paint is to soak a sponge in a wide dish containing watered-down paint.*

Making collages: *Various materials can be used (cloth, paper in different colors and textures, stickers in different colors and shapes, wool, toothpicks, beans, pasta, coffee, and so on).*

Covering holes with transparent materials: *Waxed paper or cellophane wrap can be used. The glue must always be spread on the back around the hole in the oaktag to avoid staining or wrinkling the cellophane or paper.*

Making balls: *Balls can be made with tissue paper. Tear a piece of tissue paper and wrinkle it into a ball with your fingertips. This technique exercises the children's fine motor skills by making them pinch with their finger-tips (using their index finger and thumb). When gluing, spread the glue on the surface of the oaktag and then stick the balls on. If the ball is very small, put the glue directly on the ball instead of on the oaktag.*

Methodology

The methodology presented here, based on the authors' professional experience, is useful for directing artistic activities in the classroom with children of this age group.

The most important factor will be organizing the classroom and planning the activity and the materials. You, the teacher, will have to know exactly which materials will be necessary for each session and what procedure should be followed to direct the children in each activity. Before beginning to work with the material and carry out the tasks, the children should understand what they are about to do and why, in order to motivate them and catch their interest. They should be encouraged and each theme should be placed in context in order to attain the desired educational goals. They should understand that everything they do has a purpose and can be used in other situations, that the work to be carried out is not an isolated activity but forms part of the real world. That is why the activities have a global focus; therefore, stress how the activity relates to the real world before beginning it.

Once the children's curiosity and desire to discover new things have been awakened, you can show them what the finished piece (which you will have already made as an example) will look like.

To achieve positive results, it is important to choose the right time for the activity and spread it out over more than one sitting. At this age, children tire quickly of doing the same thing for too long; therefore, depending on the duration and complexity, the activity will have to be spread out over several class sessions in order to be more relaxing and fun.

It is recommended that the activity be done first thing in the morning or afternoon, when the children are more receptive, relaxed, and rested. The interests and moods of the children must be seriously considered before starting the activity. If you see that they are restless and cannot concentrate, you may want to put it off until another time. You should avoid making the mistake of forcing the situation, since then the children would not really enjoy the activity and the results would not be so positive.

Depending on the number of children in the class and on their personalities (restless, receptive, relaxed), on the difficulty of the technique being used, or if it is the first time it has been introduced, you should either work with the entire class at one time or with small groups. In each exercise, you will find some guidelines that should be followed when teaching all of the children at once or in small groups.

When you are working with a small group, the rest of the class should be involved in some activity that does not require adult help, so that you can fully concentrate on teaching the group.

On the other hand, when working with the entire class, the activity will probably be more guided; therefore, the most important factor will be knowing how to keep their attention. The children will have to listen closely to your instructions in order to correctly carry out the activity.

Participating too actively in the children's work should be avoided, as this reduces their independence. Do not be too preoccupied with a piece's perfection; make sure that the children play and experiment with the different techniques and materials, fully enjoying them.

If it is an activity the children can do alone, it will not be necessary to guide them so much, even when working with the class as a whole. The important thing is to allow them to express themselves freely. Allow them their creativity.

If the materials to be used are very specific, these should be handed out to each child. If not, place a container in the middle of each table so the materials are easily accessible to everyone. This will help the children learn to share.

Once the class is finished, it is important to have the children realize that they must clean and put away their work utensils, as well as take care of their personal hygiene. During class, they must treat the tools and materials respectfully.

The majority of the techniques presented throughout this book can be modified to suit the children's level; for instance, if an activity calls for punching techniques, cutting can be substituted if the children are older, and so on. By the same token, the basic idea can be used, but with different techniques according to your own creativity and personal motivation and the materials available.

This book was designed to serve as a practical work tool, since it is based on the real-life experiences of three elementary school teachers. We hope their guidelines and advice will make your teaching easier and more diverse in the area of artistic expression. The presentation of each activity will help make the work more pleasant and fun so you and the children can fully enjoy it.

How the Book Is Organized

This book is organized to take into account the different ages of the children in this grade. The activities are classified according to their degree of difficulty. The classification is made according to classroom experience. All of these activities have been tested in the classroom on children of this age group. It should be noted, however, that these classifications, though, are only intended to get you started, since we are dealing with open suggestions for activities that can be modified to suit the specific needs of each group; the same activity could be modified for different age groups by making it more or less complex.

Included are both two- and three-dimensional projects. Each activity includes a list of materials needed, the degree of difficulty (from one to three), guidelines for the teacher (how to do it), steps to follow divided into sessions, and some advice on how to make everything run more smoothly.

Each step is accompanied by a photograph or an illustration to facilitate comprehension.

Summer

In this book we offer manual activities that contain various elements typical of the summer season—the beach, the sun, refreshments, leisure time—that could be used to end the course in an enjoyable fashion.

Toward the end of the school year, children will be better prepared to carry out more difficult projects, since their skills and manual dexterity will have been improving throughout the year.

Since summer coincides with school vacation, it could be a good time for parents to have fun teaching their children some of the projects in this book. The book can also serve as a handy resource for summer camp counselors or leaders of recreational groups who are working with children.

1 SAILBOAT 1

What materials are needed?

- Blue oaktag
- Glossy colored paper in various colors
- Yellow and blue finger paint
- Flat red toothpick
- Scissors
- Awl and felt pad
- Glue stick
- Paintbrush
- Template (see page 43)

How can the activity be done?

This activity can be done in three sessions of approximately half an hour each. You can work with the entire class at one time, since this activity can be easily supervised, although the last session should be done in small groups.

Session 1

For each child, prepare:
- *A sheet of blue oaktag with the outlines of the waves already drawn on it in pencil and that of the boat hull in marker*
- *A paintbrush*
- *Green and orange sheets of glossy paper with the outlines of the sails already drawn on them*

For each table, prepare:
- *A jar of blue paint*

1 **Paint the waves blue by following the outlines with your paintbrush.**

2 *Punch out the sails.*

Which techniques will be practiced?

- *Finger painting* • *Painting with a brush* • *Punching holes*
- *Cutting and pasting glossy paper* • *Pasting toothpicks*

Session 2

For each child, prepare:
- *The painted oaktag—the paint should be dry*
- *Scissors*
- *Glue*

For each table, prepare:
- *Pieces of glossy paper in different colors*

3 Cut the glossy paper into small pieces and glue them onto the boat.

Practical Advice

- **Cutting paper:** *If the children do not yet know how to use scissors well, they can be given the glossy paper already cut.*
- **Red toothpicks:** *If there are no red toothpicks available, an ordinary toothpick can be colored beforehand with crayons, markers, or paint.*
- **Punching out the sails:** *Since painting the waves will not take very long, use the first session to punch out the sails as well. Write each child's name on them for the next session.*

Teaching Suggestions

- *Work on* **fine motor skills** *when having the children follow the waves with the brush.*
- *Work on* **symmetry** *when pasting the sails in place. A project can be done first to practice this with other shapes.*

Session 3

For each child, prepare:
- *The oaktag with the partially created sailboat*
- *The punched-out sails*
- *A flat red toothpick*
- *Glue*

For each table, prepare:
- *A jar of yellow paint*

4 Glue the sails symmetrically above the boat hull, with the toothpick between them.

5 Paint a sun with your fingers in the upper corner of the picture.

2 UNDERWATER SCENE

What materials are needed?

- *Blue oaktag*
- *Blue and green tissue paper*
- *Magazines*
- *Scissors*
- *Glue stick*
- *Varnish and paintbrush*

How can the activity be done?

This activity can be done in two sessions of approximately half an hour each, working with the entire class at one time. The second session can also be done in small groups in an "art corner" if desired.

Session 1

For each child, prepare:
- *A sheet of blue oaktag*
- *A sheet each of blue and green tissue paper*
- *Glue*
- *Paintbrush*

For each table, prepare:
- *A jar of varnish*

1 **Tear the tissue paper into strips with your fingers and glue them onto the oaktag in overlapping layers to make the waves of the sea.**

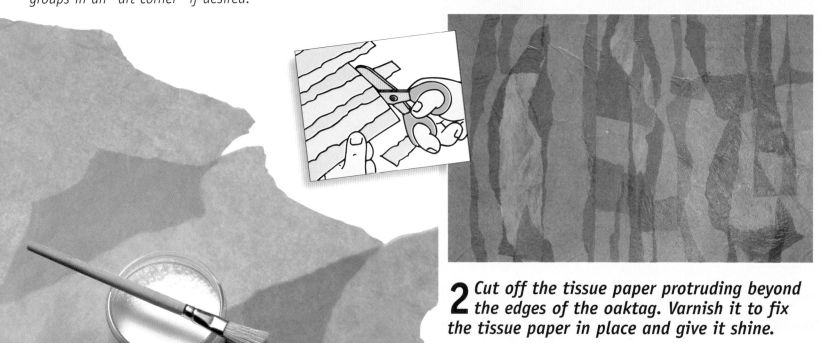

2 **Cut off the tissue paper protruding beyond the edges of the oaktag. Varnish it to fix the tissue paper in place and give it shine.**

Which techniques will be practiced?

• *Tearing tissue paper*
• *Cutting and pasting magazine pictures (collage)* • *Varnishing*

Session 2

For each child, prepare:

• *The oaktag with the varnished tissue paper on it*
• *Magazines*
• *Scissors*
• *Glue*

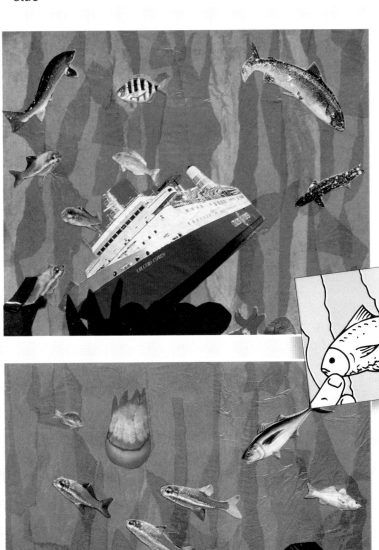

3 Look through the magazines for underwater
scenes. Cut them out and paste them onto
the background anywhere you'd like.

Practical Advice

• **Pasting tissue paper:** *The strips of tissue paper should cover the entire sheet of oaktag, and the two colors should alternate to give a more natural, less uniform appearance. Having the strips overlap adds a feeling of depth and movement.*
• **Varnishing:** *The varnish should be spread onto the entire sheet of oaktag with brush strokes in the same direction as the strips.*
• **Cutting:** *When cutting the pictures from the magazines, try to follow the outlines very closely.*
• **Collage:** *The picture can also be decorated with seaweed made of waxed paper.*

Teaching Suggestions

• *Concentrate on improving the cutting skills used when* **following the outlines** *of small objects in the magazine pictures. The smaller the object, the more control is needed to cut it out, exercising the child's fine motor skills.*
• *Work on the* **paper-tearing** *technique, pinching with the tips of the fingers.*
• *Comment on the effects of the varnish on the tissue paper (***shiny***,* **smooth***, and so on).*
• *Talk with the children about things found on the* **ocean floor** *(fish, plants, rocks), and the role of the* **undersea diver***.*

3 BUMBLEBEE

Session 1

For each child, prepare:
- *A sheet of oaktag with two bee outlines drawn on it*
- *A black wax crayon*
- *Awl and felt pad*

1 **Paint the two outlines of the bee with the black wax crayon.**

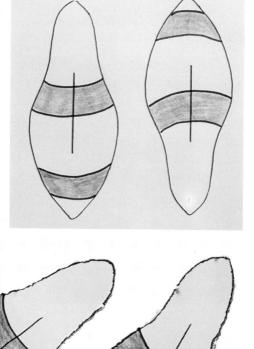

What materials are needed?

- *Yellow oaktag*
- *Green crepe paper*
- *Small, round blue stickers*
- *Two flat toothpicks*
- *Black wax crayons*
- *Awl and felt pad*
- *Glue stick*
- *Template (see page 42)*

How can the activity be done?

This activity can be done in three sessions of approximately half an hour each, working with the entire class at one time.

2 **Punch the two bee shapes out of the oaktag.**

Practical Advice

- **Pasting toothpicks:** *After pasting on the toothpicks, it is important to have the children wash their hands in order to avoid staining the yellow oaktag.*
- **Mobile:** *This bee is perfect for a mobile. It can be hung on a string to decorate the classroom.*
- **Crepe paper:** *You can use different-colored crepe paper for more colorful results.*

Which techniques will be practiced?
- *Painting with wax crayons*
- *Punching shapes out* • *Gluing*

For each child, prepare:
- *The cut-out bee shapes*
- *Two flat toothpicks*
- *Glue*
- *Two round blue stickers*

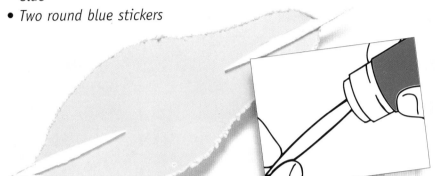

3 Spread glue onto one side of each toothpick and glue them onto the back of one of the bee halves, one on each end.

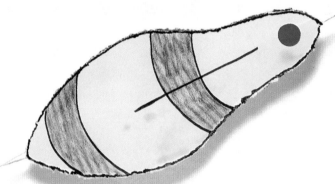

4 Spread glue onto the back of the other bee half and stick it onto the one with the toothpicks so that they are perfectly matched up. Apply the round stickers for eyes.

Teaching Suggestions
- *Explain the **life cycle of bees** and how they make honey.*
- *Ask each child to bring a jar of honey to class to observe the **different types of honey**.*
- *Take the opportunity to eat a honey and toast **snack** together.*

For each child, prepare:
- *The bee from the last session*
- *A piece of crepe paper of about a palm's length*
- *Awl and felt pad*

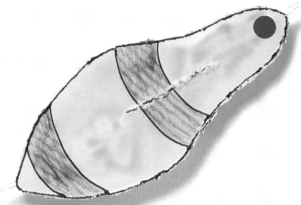

5 With the awl, punch along the black line in the middle of the bee so that the holes go all the way through both sides.

6 Slip the piece of crepe paper, folded lengthwise, through the hole, and then open it out so the wings are extended.

4 THE SUN

What materials are needed?

• *Blue oaktag*
• *Yellow finger paint*
• *Two large, round blue stickers, two small green ones, and two small red ones*
• *A large red triangular sticker*
• *Eight flat yellow toothpicks*
• *Glue stick*
• *Template (see page 47)*

How can the activity be done?

This activity can be done in three sessions of approximately half an hour each, working with the entire class at one time, since the activity can be easily supervised.

Session 1

For each child, prepare:
• *A sheet of blue oaktag with a sun drawn on it*
For each table, prepare:
• *A pan containing yellow finger paint*

1 **Paint in the sun with your fingers and the yellow finger paint.**

Teaching Suggestions

• *Emphasize the **facial features**: List the names of each part of the face and talk about where they are located.*
• *Point out the difference between **day and night**. Explain that the sun shines during the day.*
• *Have a conversation with the children about **activities that can be done in summer** in the sun.*
• *Make the children aware of the difference between the **sun's rays** in summer and in winter.*

Which techniques will be practiced?

- *Painting with finger paints*
- *Gluing toothpicks* • *Putting round stickers on oaktag*

Session 2

For each child, prepare:
- *The oaktag with the dried painted sun on it*
- *The colored stickers*

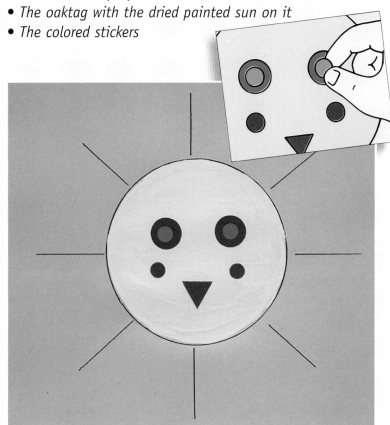

2 **Put on the round blue stickers to make the eyes, and on top of them the green ones for the pupils. Use the red ones to make the cheeks, and the triangle for the mouth.**

Practical Advice

- **Gluing toothpicks:** *Remind the children how to glue toothpicks, putting the glue on the toothpick and not on the oaktag, and holding it by the ends so as not to get too dirty.*
- **Yellow toothpicks:** *If there are no yellow toothpicks, ordinary ones can be colored with paint, crayons, or marker.*

Session 3

For each child, prepare:
- *The oaktag with the sun on it*
- *The yellow toothpicks*
- *Glue*

3 **Glue the toothpicks around the sun on the lines to make the rays.**

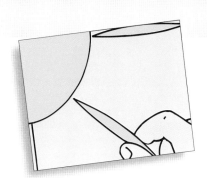

5 REFRESHMENT

What materials are needed?

- Pink oaktag
- Yellow, orange, blue, and green glossy paper
- Green cellophane or waxed paper
- Orange tissue paper
- A medium-sized round blue sticker and a small yellow one
- Orange feather
- Drinking straw
- Wooden skewer
- Transparent tape
- Awl and felt pad
- Glue stick
- Template (see page 45)

How can the activity be done?

This activity can be done in three sessions of approximately half an hour each, working with the entire class at one time, since the activity can be easily supervised.

Session 1

For each child, prepare:
- *A sheet of pink oaktag with the outline of a cup drawn on it*
- *A piece of green waxed paper or cellophane*
- *Awl and felt pad*
- *Glue*

1 **Punch out the shape of the glass.**

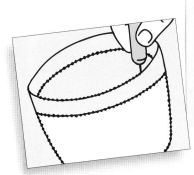

2 **Glue the green waxed paper to the back of the oaktag, making sure to cover all the holes.**

Teaching Suggestions

- *Have the children use the sense of touch to feel the **different textures** of the materials used in this activity: the different types of paper, the softness of the feather, the feel of the skewer and the straw.*
- *Play with the **straw**, blowing, sipping a drink, making soap bubbles.*

Which techniques will be practiced?
- *Wrinkling paper* • *Putting stickers on oaktag* • *Gluing waxed paper*
- *Using glue and transparent tape* • *Punching holes with an awl*

Session 2

For each child, prepare:
- *The oaktag with the glass cut out of it*
- *Different-colored sheets of glossy paper*
- *Scissors*
- *Glue*

3 Cut the glossy paper into small pieces and glue them along the rim of the glass to look like a mosaic.

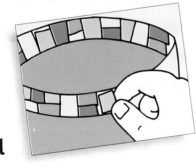

Practical Advice

- *Making a hole in the waxed paper:* Be very careful when making the hole in the waxed paper with the awl and putting the straw through, since this paper tears easily. Adult assistance may be necessary when putting tape in the back to reinforce the hole and keep the paper from tearing.
- *Transparent tape:* In this case, tape is better than glue because you do not need to wait until it dries.

Session 3

For each child, prepare:
- *The oaktag with the finished glass on it*
- *A piece of blue glossy paper with the outline of a parrot on it*
- *An orange feather*
- *Orange tissue paper (a square of approximately 2.5 inches)*
- *The yellow and blue stickers*
- *A skewer*
- *A drinking straw*

4 Punch the parrot out of the glossy paper.

5 Put the yellow sticker onto the parrot to make the eye, then glue the skewer onto the reverse side of the parrot, and the feather as a tail.

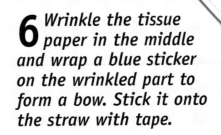

6 Wrinkle the tissue paper in the middle and wrap a blue sticker on the wrinkled part to form a bow. Stick it onto the straw with tape.

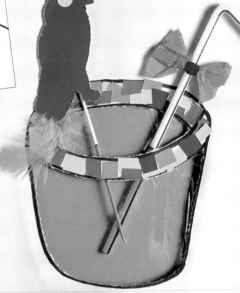

7 Make two holes in the waxed paper with the awl and put the straw and the skewer through them.

17

6 FISH

What materials are needed?

- *Purple oaktag*
- *Salt*
- *Orange, green, red, blue, and yellow rectangular sticks of chalk*
- *Aluminum foil*
- *Blue tissue paper*
- *Several sheets of paper*
- *Glue stick*
- *Template (see page 44)*

How can the activity be done?

This activity can be done in three sessions of approximately half an hour each. The teacher can work with the entire class at one time or with small groups in an "art corner," as preferred.

Session 1

For each child, prepare:
- *A sheet of purple oaktag with the outline of a fish drawn on it*
- *Blue tissue paper*
- *Aluminum foil*
- *Glue*

For each table, prepare:
- *Two trays to hold the balls*

1 **Make balls out of tissue paper and aluminum foil and place them in the trays.**

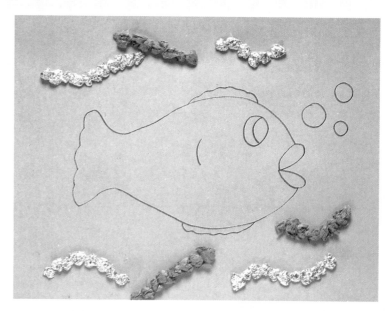

2 **Glue the balls at random onto the oaktag to make waves.**

Which techniques will be practiced?
- *Making balls with tissue paper and aluminum foil*
- *Gluing salt and balls* • *Dyeing salt*

Session 2

For each table, prepare:
- *A dish of salt*
- *A piece of colored chalk for each child (each table should dye the salt a different color; therefore, there should be five tables)*
- *A sheet of paper for each child*

3 **Spread the salt onto each child's paper and rub the chalk on it to "dye" it. When the salt is colored enough, put it back into the dish.**

Practical Advice

- ***Gluing salt:*** *Before changing colors, lift the oaktag and let the excess salt fall into the dish to avoid it mixing with the next color. After sprinkling salt over the glue-filled area, pat it gently with your fingers to make it stick better.*

Teaching Suggestions

- *Work on the **sense of touch** with materials that are new to the children, when touching the salt or making aluminum foil balls.*
- *Discuss other uses of **salt**, in addition to seasoning food.*
- *Teach how to **"dye" salt** in order to use it in other activities.*

Session 3

For each child, prepare:
- *The oaktag with the balls glued on it*
- *Glue*

For each table, prepare:
- *Five dishes with the dyed salt, each a different color*

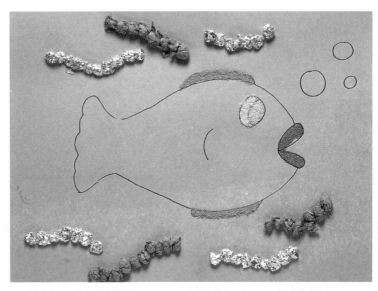

4 **Glue the salt on, sprinkling it with your fingers. Make the fins orange, the mouth red, and the eye blue and white (using regular salt for the white).**

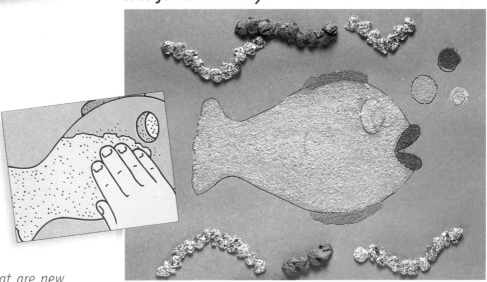

5 **Spread the glue onto the body of the fish and sprinkle on the green salt. Then fill in the bubbles with yellow, red, and white (not dyed) salt.**

7 WATERMELON

Session 1

For each child, prepare:
- *A sheet of white oaktag*
- *Red glossy paper with the outline of a slice of watermelon drawn on it*
- *Glue*
- *Scissors or awl and felt pad*

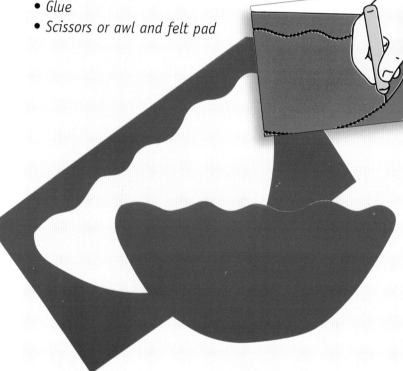

What materials are needed?

- *White oaktag*
- *Red glossy paper*
- *Small rectangular yellow and green stickers*
- *Black plasticine*
- *Scissors or awl and felt pad*
- *Glue stick*
- *Template (see page 46)*

How can the activity be done?

This activity can be done in three sessions of approximately half an hour each, working with the entire class at one time.

1 Cut or punch out the watermelon shape from the red glossy paper.

2 Glue the watermelon cutout onto the oaktag wherever you like.

Which techniques will be practiced?
• *Cutting or punching* • *Modeling clay*
• *Using colored stickers*

Session 2

For each child, prepare:
• *The oaktag with the watermelon glued on it*
• *The colored stickers*

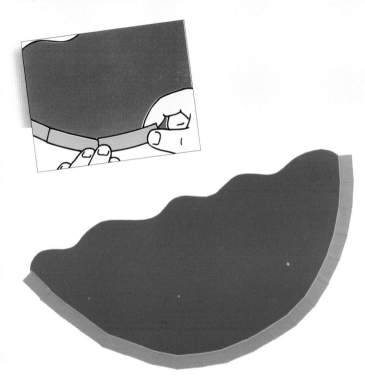

3 **Place the green rectangular stickers along the bottom edge of the watermelon.**

4 **Overlap the yellow stickers on the green ones to create the rind.**

Session 3

For each child, prepare:
• *The oaktag with the watermelon shape and the stickers on it*
• *Black plasticine*

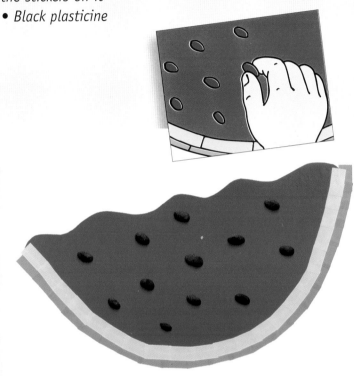

5 **Make small balls with the plasticine and stick them onto the glossy paper, making them a little oblong so that they look like seeds.**

Teaching Suggestions

• *Discuss the **different types of fruit** available in summer: Have the children name all the ones they can think of. Take the opportunity to visit a grocery store or farm stand, buy some fruit, and try it.*

Practical Advice

• ***Placing stickers:*** *The stickers should be placed so that they overlap onto each other and onto the red paper, leaving no empty spaces between them.*

8 SAILBOAT 2

Session 1

For each child, prepare:
- A sheet of blue oaktag with waves drawn on it
- A piece of blue tissue paper
- Glue

What materials are needed?

- Blue oaktag
- Orange and green glossy paper
- Blue tissue paper
- A flat toothpick
- A small, round yellow sticker
- Scissors or awl and felt pad
- Glue stick
- Varnish and brush

How can the activity be done?

This activity can be done in three sessions of approximately half an hour each, working with the entire class at one time, since the activity can be easily supervised.

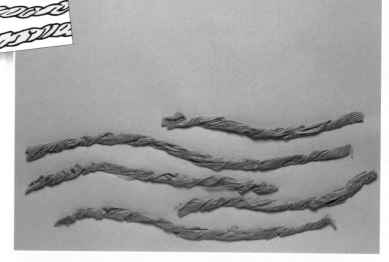

1 *Tear the tissue paper into strips and roll them like sausages. Glue them onto the lower part of the oaktag following the lines of the waves.*

Teaching Suggestions

- Work on the **rotating movement** of the wrist when rolling the tissue paper.
- Discuss what the **sail** is for: to direct the boat with the help of the wind.

Which techniques will be practiced?

- *Tearing tissue paper*
- *Cutting and gluing glossy paper (collage)* • *Varnishing*

Session 2

For each child, prepare:
- *Orange glossy paper with the sail outlines already drawn on it*
- *Green glossy paper with the boat already drawn on it*
- *Scissors or awl and felt pad*

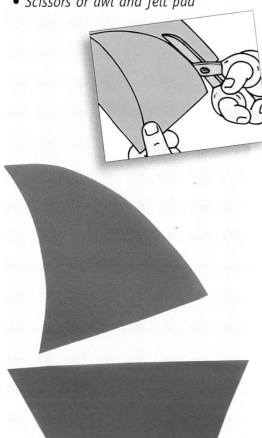

2 Cut or punch out the sail and hull.

Practical Advice

- **Puncturing the sail:** *If a child has trouble sticking the toothpick through the sail, you will have to help.*
- **Gluing the rolls:** *When gluing the rolls of tissue paper on as waves, it will be necessary to press and hold them in place for several seconds in order for them to stick well.*

Session 3

For each child, prepare:
- *The oaktag with the waves glued on it*
- *The glossy paper cutouts of sail and hull*
- *A toothpick*
- *Glue*
- *A round yellow sticker*

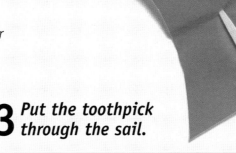

3 Put the toothpick through the sail.

4 Glue the green glossy paper hull above the waves. Then glue only the toothpick part of the sail to give the sail more volume and dimension.

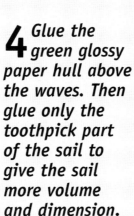

5 Put on the yellow sticker to make the sun.

9 JEWELRY BOX

Single Session

For each child, prepare:
• A stick of brown plasticine
• Seashells
• A paintbrush

For each table, prepare:
• A jar of varnish

What materials are needed?

• Brown plasticine
• Seashells
• Varnish and brush

1 *Make a ball of plasticine using the whole stick.*

How can the activity be done?

This activity can be done in a single half-hour session, working with the entire class at one time, since the activity can be easily supervised.

2 *Make a cavity in the center with your fingers and keep deepening it. Shape it to look like a jewelry box and smooth the sides.*

Which techniques will be practiced?

• *Modeling plasticine*
• *Varnishing* • *Decorating with seashells*

Teaching Suggestions

• *Discuss the* **use of the jewelry box**—*who can use it, and so on.*
• *Encourage* **creativity** *by letting the children place the shells at random and shape the jewelry box into any shape they like—round, oval, and so on.*
• *Note the* **utility of the plasticine**. *It is almost as good as clay for making objects, as well as being fun to play with and useful for filling in spaces.*

Practical Advice

• *Varnishing: It is important to use a generous amount of varnish to cover the entire jewelry box, especially the seashells, since, in addition to making the box harder, it will also keep the shells fixed in the plasticine. It will not be necessary to varnish the base.*
• *Name: Each child's name can be written on the base with an awl to keep from mixing up the boxes.*
• *Seashells: The seashells can be placed close together, but they should not touch each other so that they stick better.*

3 *Stick the seashells along the walls of the jewelry box, applying a bit of pressure. Varnish.*

10 POPSICLE

What materials are needed?

- Blue oaktag
- Yellow and orange tissue paper
- Multicolored shavings from wax crayons
- Flat wooden popsicle stick
- Awl and felt pad
- Glue stick
- Varnish and paintbrush
- Template (see page 42)

How can the activity be done?

This activity can be done in two sessions of approximately half an hour each, working with the entire class at one time.

Session 1

For each child, prepare:
- *A sheet of blue oaktag with the outline of a popsicle drawn on it*
- *Two pieces of tissue paper: one yellow and the other orange*
- *Awl and felt pad*
- *Glue*

1 **Punch out the top and bottom parts of the popsicle from the oaktag.**

2 **Glue the yellow tissue paper onto the back of the oaktag to cover the upper hole, and the orange one to cover the lower hole.**

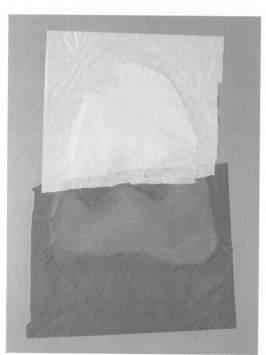

Which techniques will be practiced?

- *Punching out shapes* • *Gluing tissue paper*
- *Gluing wax shavings*

For each child, prepare:
- *The oaktag with the tissue paper glued onto it*
- *Popsicle stick*
- *Glue*
- *Paintbrush*

For each table, prepare:
- *A dish containing the wax shavings*
- *A jar of varnish*

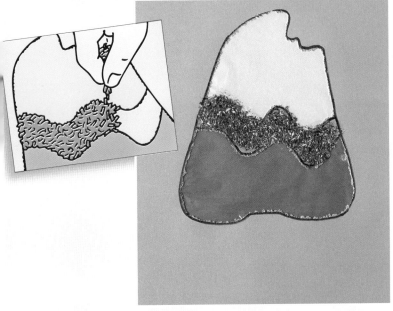

3 **Glue the wax shavings onto the central strip of the popsicle, sprinkling them on with your fingers. Varnish.**

4 **Glue the popsicle stick onto the oaktag below the popsicle.**

Practical Advice

- **Wax shavings:** *It is a good idea to have the children sharpen the crayons themselves to make the shavings, so they can see how something we normally throw away can be recycled as decoration.*
- **Gluing wax shavings:** *Once the shavings have been sprinkled over the glue, pat them down and lift the oaktag to get rid of any excess shavings.*

Teaching Suggestions

- *Discuss the different **states of water:** liquid, solid, and gas. Comment on its properties.*

11 CATERPILLAR

What materials are needed?

- Four small plastic yogurt containers
- Blue, green, yellow, and red finger paint
- Thick red yarn
- Two flat toothpicks
- Two light blue paper balls
- A styrofoam ball
- Three small round stickers—two blue and one red
- A wide paintbrush
- A large plastic needle
- Liquid dishwashing detergent

Prepare four tables with:
- *A jar of paint of a different color for each table, mixed with some dishwashing detergent*
- *A paintbrush for each child*

Prepare another table where the children can leave the painted yogurt containers

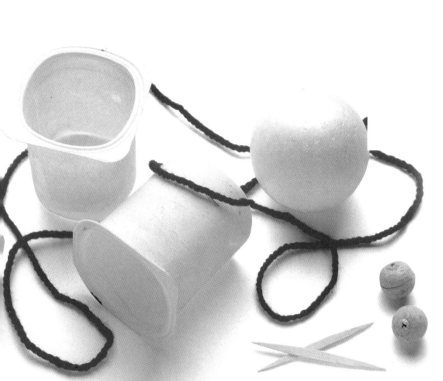

1 **Paint four yogurt containers with the paintbrush, each one a different color.**

How can the activity be done?

This activity can be done in two sessions of approximately half an hour each, working with the entire class at one time, since the activity can be easily supervised. During the first session, it is a good idea to have a different color paint at each table. When the children finish painting one yogurt container, they can move on to the next table and start painting a different one in a new color, and so on until they have been to all of the tables. If a table is full, they should wait until someone finishes.

Which techniques will be practiced?

- *Using a paintbrush* • *Threading a needle and pushing it through an object*
- *Putting on colored stickers* • *Poking toothpicks into styrofoam*

Session 2

For each child, prepare:
- *The four painted yogurt containers*
- *Two flat toothpicks*
- *Two small paper balls*
- *A styrofoam ball*
- *Three stickers—two blue and one red*
- *A large plastic needle*
- *A string of red yarn*

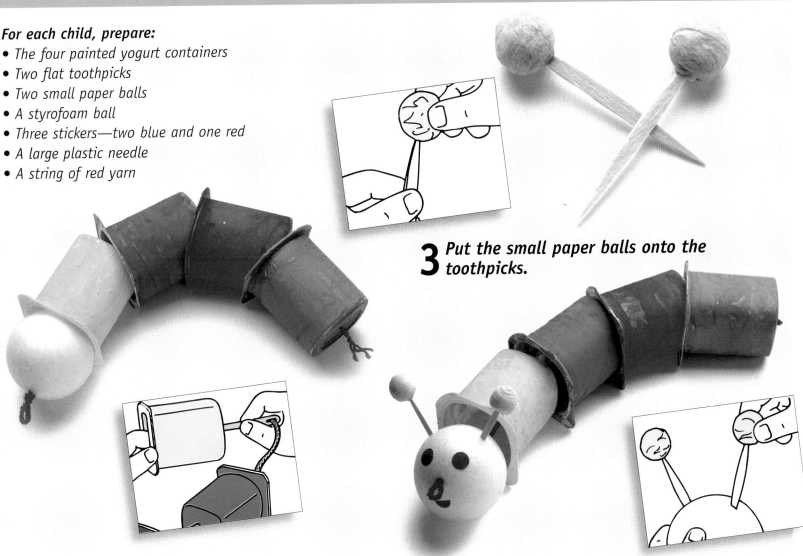

3 **Put the small paper balls onto the toothpicks.**

2 **Thread the needle with the yarn, knot the ends, and stick it through the bottoms of the four yogurt cups and then through the styrofoam ball. Make a knot at this end now.**

4 **Stick the toothpicks into the styrofoam ball to make the antennas. Put the blue stickers onto the ball to make the eyes, and the red one for the mouth.**

Practical Advice

- ***Painting:*** *The paint will probably slide off the plastic. To avoid this, add liquid dishwashing detergent and mix. This will help the paint stay on the plastic.*
- ***Threading the needle:*** *When working with children who have little practice in threading a needle and tying the ends of the yarn, divide the class into small groups to guide and help those who are having trouble.*
- ***Balls of paper:*** *If they are not available on the market, balls can be made from tissue paper or plasticine.*

Teaching Suggestions

- *Introduce **mathematical concepts** such as spherical shapes.*
- *Comment on the life cycle of the **caterpillar** and how it changes. Discuss its natural habitat and its way of life.*

29

12 SEASHORE

What materials are needed?

- Blue oaktag
- Blue tissue paper
- Glossy paper in various colors
- Sawdust
- Seashells
- Awl and felt pad
- Varnish and paintbrush
- Glue stick
- Template (see page 45)

How can the activity be done?

This activity can be done in three sessions of approximately half an hour each, working with the entire class at one time, since the activity can be easily supervised.

Session 1

For each child, prepare:
- A sheet of blue oaktag with a line drawn on it to separate the sea and the shore
- Glue

For each table, prepare:
- A dish containing sawdust

1 **Put glue on the half representing the shore and sprinkle the sawdust on with your fingers. Allow it to dry.**

Teaching Suggestions

- Experiment first with the **sawdust**. Touch it to feel its texture, talk about its uses and how similar it is to the sand on the beach.
- Discuss the things we need and take along when we go to the **beach**, emphasizing respect for the environment and cleanliness.
- Observe the **dangers of the beach** and how to prevent possible accidents.
- Name different **fish** that the children know. Bring in books or photographs of these and see how many they don't know. Discuss their colors and physical characteristics. You can make a mural with them.
- Talk about the **bottom of the sea** where there are not only animals, but plants as well.

Which techniques will be practiced?

• *Gluing paper* • *Tearing tissue paper into strips* • *Gluing sawdust*
• *Gluing seashells* • *Punching holes* • *Varnishing*

Session 2

For each child, prepare:
• *The oaktag with the sawdust glued on it*
• *Blue tissue paper*
• *Two seashells*
• *Glue* • *A paintbrush*

For each table, prepare:
• *A jar of varnish*

2 **With fingers, tear the tissue paper into strips and paste them, overlapping slightly to cover the entire sea area. Varnish the sawdust.**

3 **Trim the tissue paper that sticks out over the edges of the oaktag. Glue the two shells somewhere on the sawdust. Varnish everything.**

Session 3

For each child, prepare:
• *The oaktag with the sand and the sea already done*
• *Different-colored glossy paper with the outlines of fish and marine life drawn on them*
• *Awl and felt pad*
• *Glue*

4 **Punch out the figures drawn on the glossy paper.**

5 **Paste these figures at random onto the sea.**

Practical Advice

• **Gluing sawdust:** The glue should be put on generously. Once the sawdust has been evenly spread to cover the entire area, lift the oaktag to let the excess sand fall into the dish.
• **Punching holes:** The glossy paper can be folded so as to punch out two or more figures at a time.
• **Varnishing sawdust:** The paintbrush should not be dragged too much. Stroke lightly and allow the varnish to seep in.
• **Varnishing seashells:** The seashells must be varnished heavily to keep them in place.

13 KITE

Session 1

For each child, prepare:
• A sheet of blue oaktag with the outline of a kite drawn on it
• Awl and felt pad
• Glue

What materials are needed?

• Blue oaktag
• Yellow, orange, green, white, and red tissue paper
• Colored rectangular stickers
• Four flat blue toothpicks
• White shoestring
• Awl and felt pad
• Glue stick
• Scissors
• Template (see page 48)

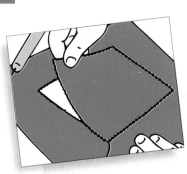

1 Punch the square out of the oaktag.

How can the activity be done?

This activity can be done in three sessions of approximately half an hour each, working with the entire class at one time, since the activity can be easily supervised.

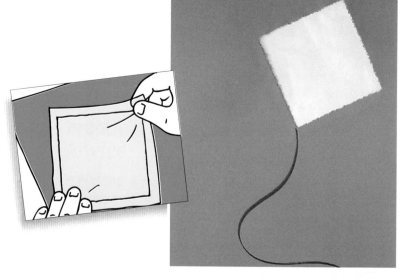

2 Glue the yellow tissue paper onto the back of the oaktag to cover the entire kite area.

Which techniques will be practiced?

- Punching holes • Cutting • Gluing tissue paper
- Attaching colored stickers • Gluing toothpicks and string

Session 2

For each child, prepare:
- *The oaktag with the tissue paper glued on it*
- *Four flat blue toothpicks*
- *The white shoestring*
- *Glue*

3 Glue the four toothpicks onto the tissue paper in the shape of an X.

4 Put glue on the line representing the tail, and glue the shoestring in place.

Session 3

For each child, prepare:
- *The oaktag with the kite from the previous session*
- *Yellow, orange, green, white, and red strips of tissue paper*
- *Colored rectangular stickers*
- *Scissors*
- *Glue*

5 Cut the strips of tissue paper into squares (about 2.5 inches) and gather them in the middle to make a bow. Use a sticker of a different color than the bow to stick around the gathered middle.

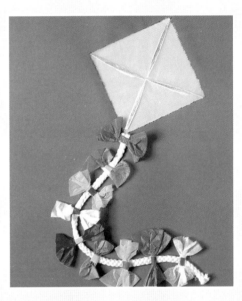

6 Glue the colored bows onto the white tail.

Teaching Suggestions

- *Concentrate on the theme of **leisure time and games**; discuss activities that the children do outside (on the beach, in the country, in a park).*
- *Bring in **a kite** and make it fly in the yard.*
- *Teach the children to **make paper bows** so they can use them in other activities.*

Practical Advice

- ***Giant size:*** *This kite can be made to actual size by the entire class and can be used to decorate the classroom.*
- ***The tail:*** *The tail can also be made of satin ribbon, which will also be attractive.*
- ***Toothpicks:*** *If there are no blue toothpicks available, an ordinary toothpick can be colored beforehand with crayons, marker, or paint.*

14 PINWHEEL

Single Session

For each child, prepare:
- *A plastic sheet with the outlines of a pinwheel drawn on it*
- *A pin with a colored round head*
- *A drinking straw*
- *A piece of an eraser*
- *Scissors*

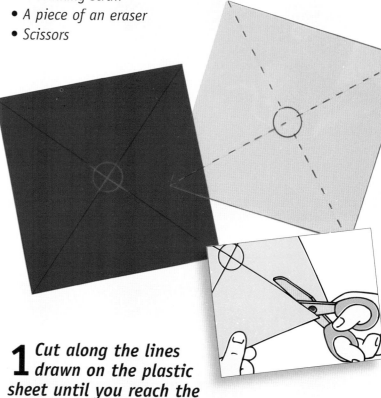

What materials are needed?

- *Colored plastic sheets (like the ones used as separators in looseleaf notebooks)*
- *Pins with round heads of different colors*
- *Erasers*
- *Drinking straws*
- *Scissors*

How can the activity be done?

This activity can be done in a single session of approximately half an hour, working in small groups so that you can supervise the children at all times.

1 **Cut along the lines drawn on the plastic sheet until you reach the circle in the center.**

Teaching Suggestions

- *Discuss **the wind** as an atmospheric phenomenon that makes the pinwheel move. Experiment with it in the schoolyard on a windy day.*
- *Demonstrate the **effect of the wind** on light objects (they move) and heavy ones (they remain static).*

Which techniques will be practiced?
- *Cutting*
- *Pinning things in place*

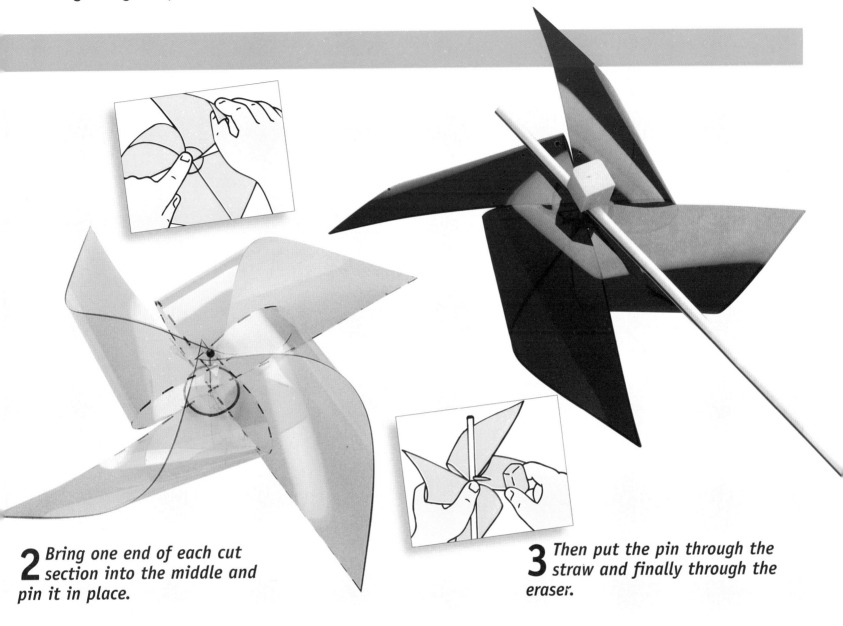

2 **Bring one end of each cut section into the middle and pin it in place.**

3 **Then put the pin through the straw and finally through the eraser.**

Practical Advice

- **Pinwheel:** *The pinwheel can also be made of glossy paper or even oaktag, although the plastic sheets are stronger and more attractive to children. It is a somewhat unusual material to them and it will be a new sensation for them to cut it.*
- **Pinning:** *Putting the pin through the various materials will require the supervision and help of an adult.*
- **Eraser:** *A piece of cork can also be used, but erasers are more readily available in a classroom.*
- **Decorating:** *You can give each child a different colored plastic sheet. The pinwheels can also be decorated with colored stickers as a finishing touch.*

35

15 ICE-CREAM CONE

What materials are needed?

- *Green oaktag*
- *Yellow, orange, brown, and white tissue paper*
- *Glue stick*
- *Template (see page 43)*

How can the activity be done?

This activity can be done in three sessions of approximately half an hour each, working with the entire class at one time, or the first session can also be done in groups, with a special corner where the children who are finished early can go before the next stage.

Session 1

For each table, prepare:
- *Three trays on which to put the different-colored balls*
- *Yellow, orange, and white tissue paper*

1 *Make balls out of the three sheets of colored tissue paper and place them in the trays, separating them by color.*

Teaching Suggestions

- *Discuss the difference between **hot and cold** food. Experience the different sensations caused by each by trying them.*
- *Make a list of possible ice cream **flavors**.*

Practical Advice

- ***Gluing strips of torn paper:*** *Any rough edges sticking up after gluing down the brown tissue paper should be no problem since they add a feeling of being three-dimensional and make the texture resemble that of a real ice-cream cone.*
- ***Scoops of ice cream:*** *The colors of the three scoops of ice cream do not have to be the same for every child. You can let them choose their colors according to their favorite flavors.*

Which techniques will be practiced?

- *Making balls with tissue paper*
- *Tearing tissue paper* • *Gluing tissue paper*

Session 2

For each child, prepare:
- *A sheet of green oaktag with the outline of an ice-cream cone drawn on it*
- *A piece of brown tissue paper*
- *Glue*

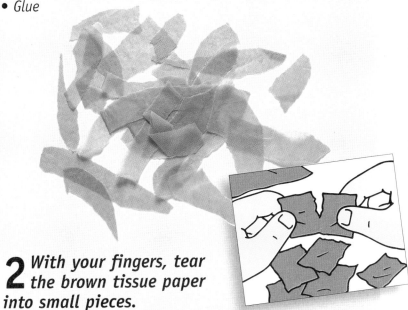

2 **With your fingers, tear the brown tissue paper into small pieces.**

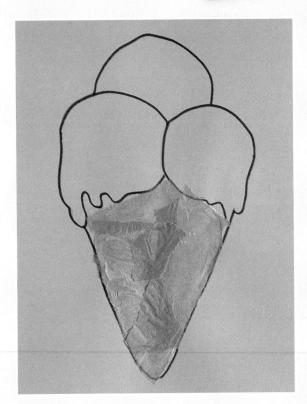

3 **Paste the pieces of tissue paper onto the ice-cream cone.**

Session 3

For each child, prepare:
- *The oaktag with the finished cone on it*
- *Glue*

For each table, prepare:
- *The three dishes containing the tissue paper balls*

4 **Glue the tissue paper balls onto the three scoop areas, with one color per scoop.**

16 THE BEACH

What materials are needed?

- *White oaktag*
- *Brown paint made of chalk*
- *Blue finger paint*
- *Varnish and paintbrush*
- *Scissors*
- *Glue stick*
- *Magazines*

How can the activity be done?

This activity can be done in three sessions of approximately half an hour each, working with the entire class at one time, although the last session could also be done in small groups in an art corner.

Session 1

For each child, prepare:
- *A sheet of white oaktag*
- *A paintbrush for spreading the paint*
- *Varnish and a paintbrush for varnishing*

For the whole group, prepare:
- *Everything necessary to make the chalk paint: rectangular colored chalk, varnish, water, paintbrush, mortar and pestle or something similar, and a bowl in which to mix everything.*

1 **Prepare chalk paint with the children's help:**
- **Break the chalk into bits and place them in a pestle or something similar and crush them, leaving some lumps.**
- **Add varnish and a very small amount of water.**
- **Mix with the paintbrush (the final texture should be lumpy or granular to add relief and resemble sand).**

2 **With the chalk paint, paint the part of the oaktag representing the sand and allow it to dry.**

Which techniques will be practiced?

• *Making and using chalk paint* • *Stamping paint with the hand*
• *Cutting and pasting magazine paper* • *Varnishing*

Session 2

For each child, prepare:
• *The oaktag with the dried "sand"*
At a table, prepare:
• *A dish containing blue finger paint*

3 **Stamp the blue finger paint onto the sea half of the oaktag with the side of your hand. Varnish the sand.**

Teaching Suggestions

• *Stimulate* **creativity** *by letting the children choose their own pictures from the magazines and having them paste them at random on the sand.*
• *Teach and improve the* **cutting method** *used when cutting the magazine pictures with the scissors.*
• *Work on* **the texture and relief** *of the sand and compare it with the result obtained with the chalk paint.*

Practical Advice

• **Stamping:** *To avoid excess paint from wetting the oaktag, dilute the paint with water.*
• **Chalk paint:** *If the chalk pieces are too difficult to crush, you can leave them soaking for a few hours in the water and varnish and crush them later.*
• **Painting:** *To create relief in the sand, you will have to use the lumps at the bottom of the paint dish, scooping them up with your paintbrush.*

Session 3

For each child, prepare:
• *The painted oaktag, dry*
• *Magazines*
• *Scissors*
• *Glue*

4 **Cut pictures of beach items out of the magazine and paste them onto the sand.**

17 FLOWERS

What materials are needed?

- *Yellow, green, pink, and white plasticine*
- *Two wooden sticks*
- *Varnish and paintbrush*

How can the activity be done?

This activity can be done in two sessions of approximately half an hour each. You can work with the entire class at one time, since the activity should be easily supervised, although the varnishing can be done in small groups.

Session 1

For each child, prepare:
- *Yellow, green, pink, and white plasticine*
- *Two wooden sticks*

1 **Make several marble-sized balls from the plasticine.**

2 **Break the sticks to the desired length and cover them completely with green plasticine.**

Teaching Suggestions

- *Emphasize **roundness**. It will be important to make perfectly round balls.*

Practical Advice

- ***Covering the sticks:*** *Have the children use their thumbs to cover the sticks completely with plasticine. Make sure there are no holes.*
- ***Washing your hands:*** *It is important to wash your hands before changing plasticine colors; otherwise, the colors will mix.*

Which techniques will be practiced?

- *Modeling plasticine*
- *Varnishing*

Session 2

For each child, prepare:
- *The pieces from the previous session*
- *A large piece of yellow plasticine*

3 **Flatten the pink balls so they are circular and look like petals. Place them around the yellow ball, using it as the center of the flower.**

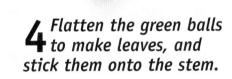

4 **Flatten the green balls to make leaves, and stick them onto the stem.**

5 **Poke the flower onto the end of the stick and varnish it. Stick it into a base made of plasticine and large enough to hold several flowers.**

6 **Repeat the process for the other flowers.**

41

TEMPLATES

What materials are needed?

- *Tracing paper*
- *Black marker*
- *Carbon paper or photocopier*

How can the activity be done?

Trace the template onto the tracing paper with the marker,
then photocopy the result onto the oaktag of the desired color.
If a photocopying machine is not available, use carbon paper to transfer the figures.

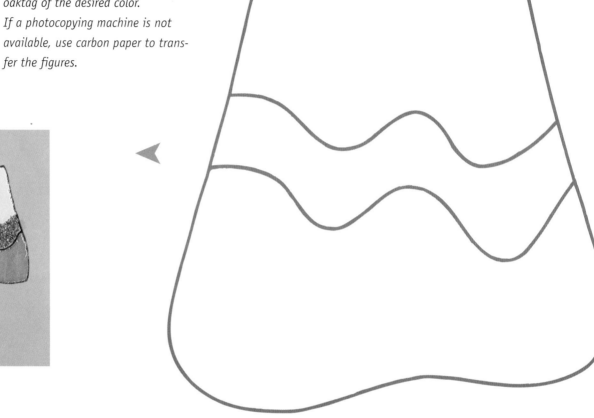

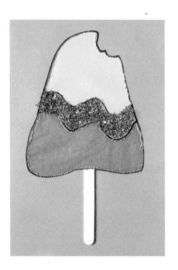

Activity 10

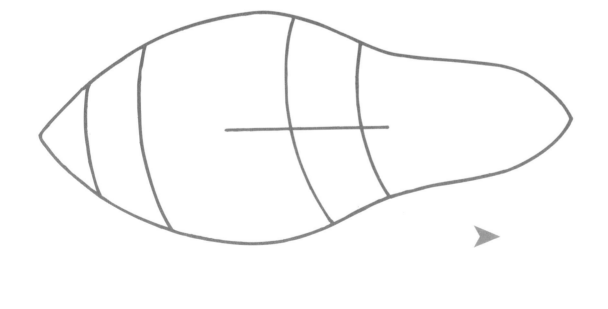

Activity 3

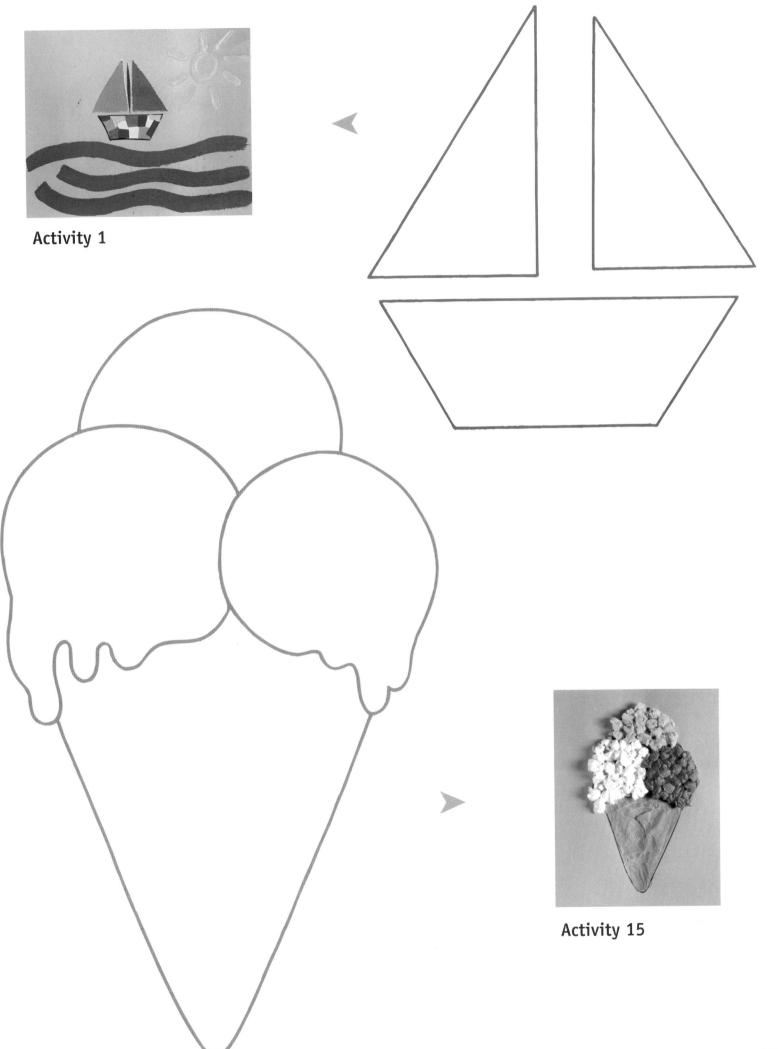

Activity 1

Activity 15

TEMPLATES

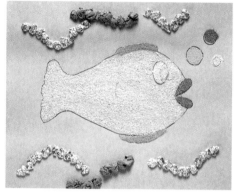

Activity 6

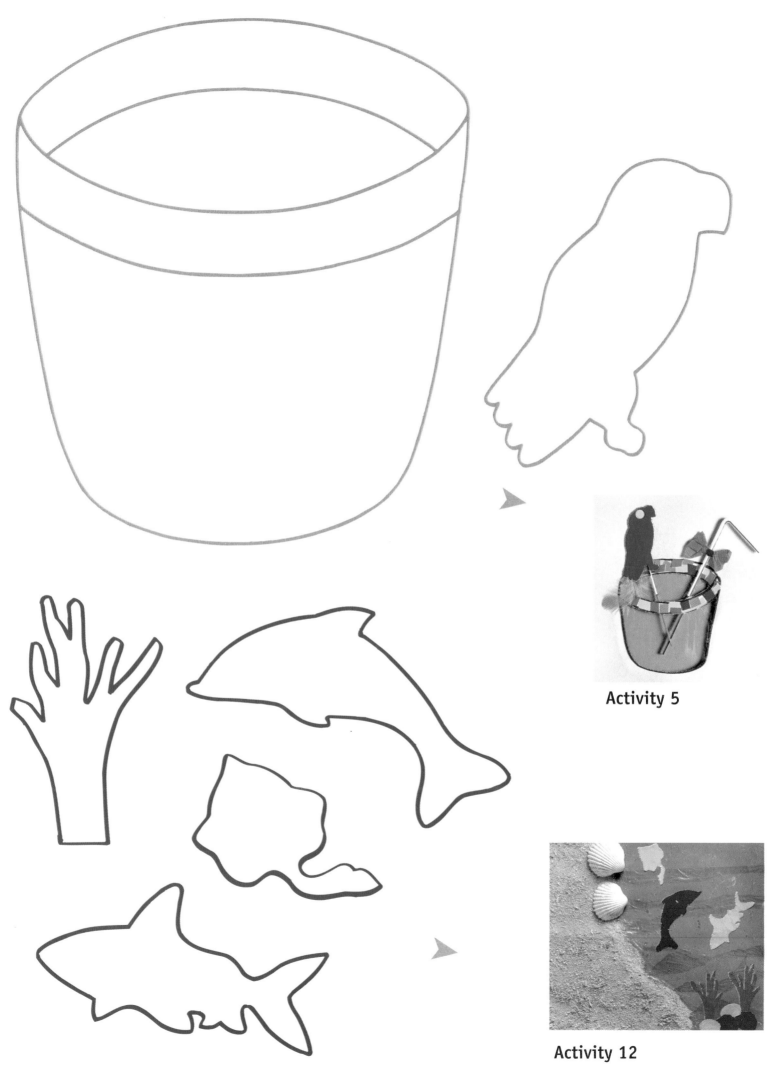

Activity 5

Activity 12

45

TEMPLATES

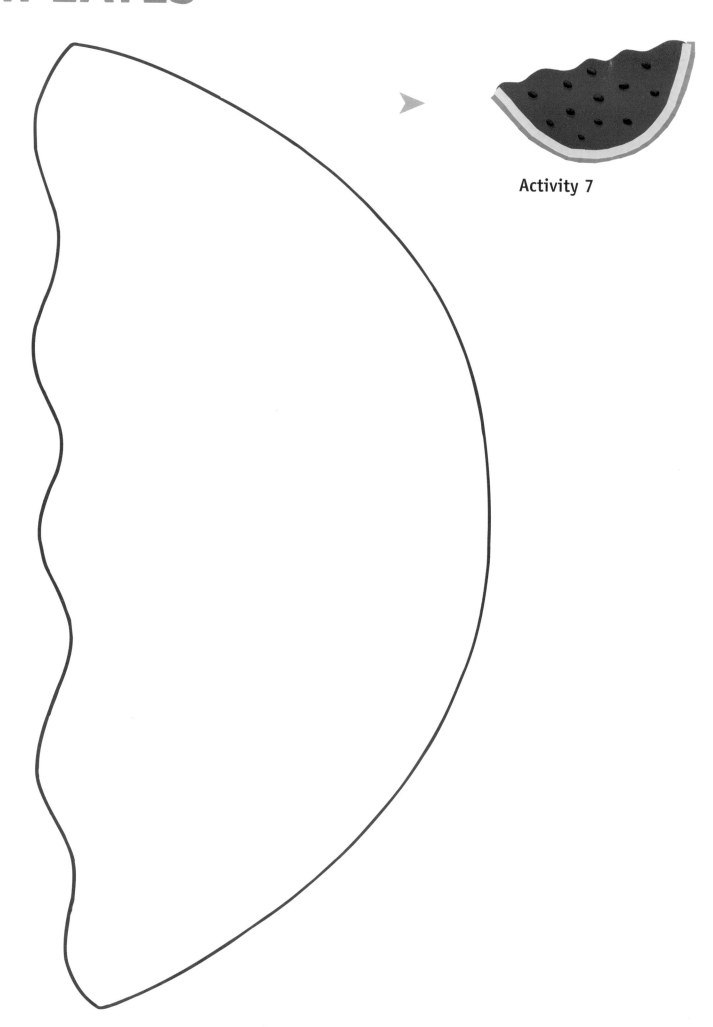

Activity 7

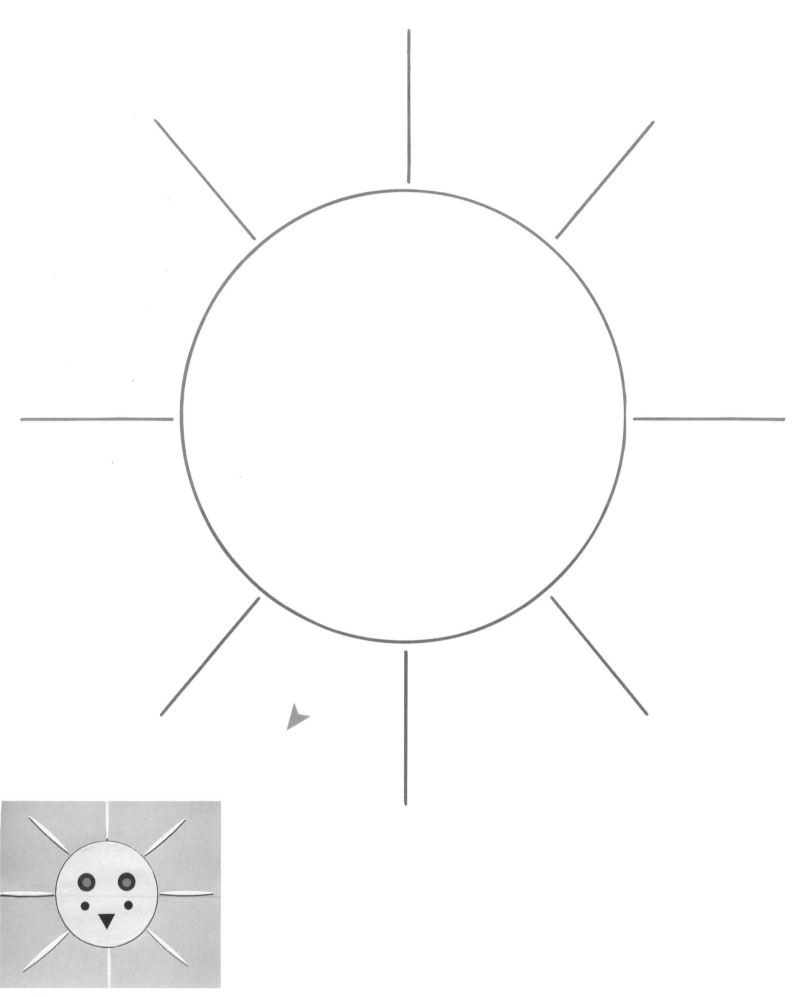

Activity 4

TEMPLATES

Activity 13

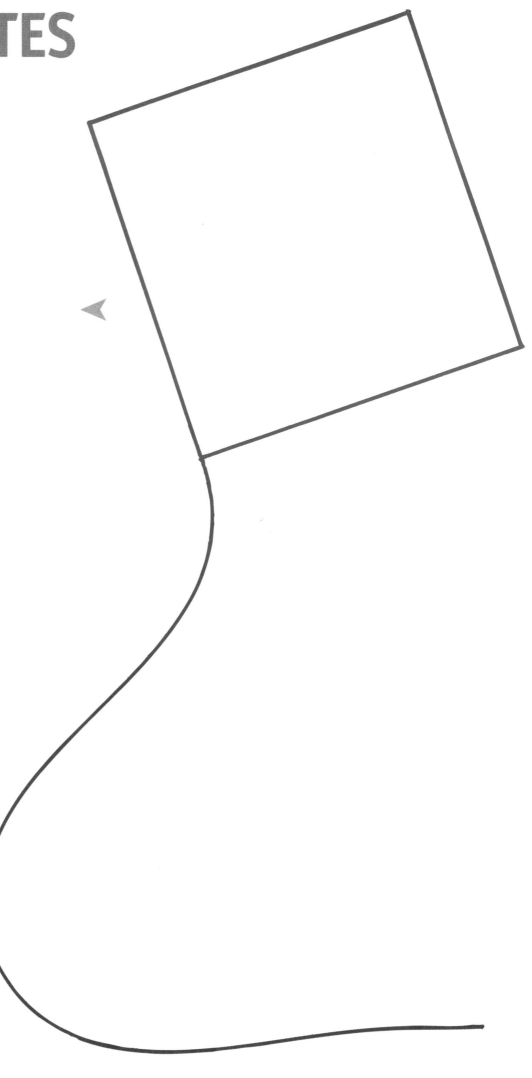